To: Katelin Rose Patterson 3-94

Printed in the U.S.A.

ISBN 0-7172-8272-4

Something Special

A Book About Love

By Michaela Muntean • Illustrated by Joel Schick

GROLIER

Fozzie Bear and his grandpa have known each other for a long time. In fact, Fozzie can't remember a time when he and his grandpa didn't do things together, or a time when he and his grandpa weren't friends.

It was Grandpa Bear who took Fozzie on his first fishing trip. Of course, Fozzie *did* get the lines all tangled up and nearly overturned the boat, but Grandpa just said, "Don't worry, Fozzie. You'll get the hang of it."

It was Grandpa Bear who taught Fozzie how to ride a two-wheeler without the training wheels. Of course, Fozzie *did* fall over a few times, but Grandpa just said, "Don't worry, Fozzie. You'll get the hang of it."

It was Grandpa Bear who gave Fozzie his first baseball and bat. Every afternoon for months, Grandpa and Fozzie practiced. Grandpa pitched and Fozzie hit. Well, sometimes he hit. Whenever Fozzie missed, Grandpa just said, "Don't worry, Fozzie. You'll get the hang of it."

Fozzie isn't a baby bear cub anymore. He's bigger and stronger, and Fozzie's grandpa was right. Fozzie *did* get the hang of just about everything. He's pretty good at fishing. He can ride a two-wheeler without training wheels, and he can hit a baseball quite a long way.

Another thing that's changed is that Fozzie doesn't spend as much time with his grandpa as he used to. Now Fozzie has other friends to go fishing and bike riding with, and he plays baseball in Little League.

One thing, however, hasn't changed. Every year, Fozzie and his grandpa have gone to the opening day game of their favorite baseball team—the Southside Sluggers.

They've always arrived early to watch batting practice. They've always brought their mitts in case a ball is hit into the stands, and they've always eaten hot dogs before, during, and after the game. Both Fozzie and his grandpa like their hot dogs with relish, onions, and mustard.

This year's opening day game was two weeks away. Fozzie and his grandpa were busy making plans.

"I'll pick you up at one o'clock," said Grandpa.

"I'll be ready," said Fozzie. "Maybe this year I'll get Sid Bearnandez's autograph!" Sid was Fozzie's favorite player.

Just as Grandpa was getting ready to leave, Kermit came running up.

"Guess what?" cried Kermit. "I've got two tickets to see the Swingling Brothers Circus! Would you like to go with me, Fozzie?"

"You bet I would," said Fozzie. "When is it?"

"Two weeks from today at one o'clock in the afternoon," Kermit answered.

"Oh," said Fozzie.

"Oh, what?" asked Kermit. "I thought you'd be excited about going."

"I am," said Fozzie. "But that's the same day my grandpa and I are going to the baseball game."

Now it was Kermit's turn to say "Oh."

Grandpa looked at Fozzie's sad face. "Why don't you go to the circus," he said. "We've been to lots of opening day games together. It won't matter if we miss one."

"Really?" asked Fozzie.

"Really," said Grandpa.

"Okay, Kermit," said Fozzie. "I'll go to the circus."

"Super," said Kermit, and off he went, happy that his best friend would be going with him.

It was time for Grandpa to go, too, so he hugged Fozzie and set off toward home.

Fozzie should have been excited about going to the circus with Kermit. But instead, he felt funny. He didn't want to miss the opening day game with Grandpa. Besides that, Grandpa hadn't even seemed to care if Fozzie went to the game or not. *Maybe Grandpa would rather go by himself*, Fozzie thought.

All through dinner, Fozzie thought about the decision he had made. He was still thinking about it as he climbed into bed that night.

First thing the next morning, Fozzie went next door to Kermit's house. "I'm sorry," he told Kermit, "but I can't go to the circus with you."

"Why not?" Kermit asked. "I thought you wanted to go."

"I do," said Fozzie. "But I already had plans with my grandpa, and I really want to go with him, too."

"I understand," said Kermit. "You're lucky to have a grandpa like yours, Fozzie."

"I know," said Fozzie as he hopped on his bike and headed for Grandpa's apartment.

"You're up bright and early, Fozzie," Grandpa
said as he opened the door for his grandson.

"I have to talk to you," Fozzie explained.

"Is something wrong?" Grandpa asked.

"Kind of...well, sort of...well, *yes*," said
Fozzie. "It's about the baseball game."

"What about it?" Grandpa asked.

"I told Kermit I couldn't go to the circus with him," Fozzie said. "I'd rather go to the baseball game with you, Grandpa...that is, if you still want me to."

"*Want* you to?" said Grandpa. "Of course I want you to! What gave you the idea I didn't?"

"Well," said Fozzie slowly, "when Kermit asked me to go to the circus, you said I should go with him. I thought maybe you didn't care if I went with you or not."

"Oh, Fozzie," Grandpa said as he put an arm around his grandson's shoulders. "Of course I care. Let me explain something to you."

"Having a grandson like you," Grandpa began, "has been one of the best things in my life. We have a very special friendship, Fozzie, and I love you very much.

"And when you love someone," Grandpa went on, "sometimes you have to let him do the things *he* wants to do instead of the things *you* want to do. Do you understand?"

"I think so," Fozzie said. "You want me to be able to make my own decisions."

"That's right," said Grandpa. "You have your own friends now. Sometimes you'll choose to do things with them rather than with me. I just wanted you to know that that's all right...and that I won't stop loving you, whatever you choose to do."

"I love you, too, Grandpa," Fozzie said. "I like choosing to do things with my friends ... but this time, I choose *you*. We really do have something special between us, don't we?"

"We sure do," said Grandpa. "And sharing something special is what love is all about, my Fozzie Bear."

Let's Talk About Love

Fozzie is really lucky to have such a wonderful grandpa, isn't he? They love each other a lot. And loving people is one of the most important things we can do.

Here are some questions about love for you to think about:

Who are the people you love?

Can you think of some ways to let them know you love them?

When people tell you that they love you, how does that make you feel?